THE MEANEST BIRTHDAY GIRL

Josh Schneider

Houghton Mifflin Harcourt

Boston New York

The text of this book was set in Binny Old Style MT.
The illustrations were executed in watercolor, pen and ink, and colored pencil.
Book design by Opal Roengchai

The Library of Congress has cataloged the hardcover edition as follows:
Schneider, Josh, 1980–
The meanest birthday girl / by Josh Schneider.
p. cm.
Summary: Dana soon learns that receiving a big white elephant for her
birthday is not as wonderful as she thought it would be.
[1. Birthdays—Fiction. 2. Gifts—Fiction. 3. Elephants—Fiction.] I. Title.
PZ7.S36335Won 2013
[E]—dc23
2011041587

ISBN: 978-0-547-83814-4 hardcover
ISBN: 978-0-544-45597-9 paperback

Manufactured in China
SCP 10 9 8 7 6 5 4 3 2 1

4500517336

To the real Dana, who is only half as
terrible as this Dana, tops

Contents

Ickaborse

It was Dana's birthday and she
could do whatever she liked.

She got dressed in her favorite
birthday dress and ate her favorite
birthday breakfast. Then she gathered
up her books and went to get on the
bus to school.

Anthony was waiting at the bus stop. It was Dana's birthday and she could do whatever she liked, and she liked to call Anthony names. She decided to call him an ickaborse.

You are an ickaborse, Anthony.

Then she pinched him
very hard. Dana also
liked to pinch.

At school, Dana showed off her
favorite birthday dress to all her
friends.

At lunch, she had two desserts in her lunch box, because it was her birthday. She ate her two desserts, and then she ate Anthony's dessert, too. Dana liked dessert.

After school, all Dana's friends came over to her house and gave her birthday presents. She got two hair ribbons and two books and three toy ponies and one doll that burped when you burped it.

After Dana had opened all her presents, her friends went home.

Then Dana ate her favorite birthday
dinner and got ready for bed.

The Wonderful Present

Dana had just gotten into her pajamas
when there was a knock at the door.
She could not imagine who it could be.
All her friends had already been by
with her birthday presents. She opened
the door. It was Anthony.

"What are you doing here, you
ickaborse?" asked Dana.

"Happy birthday, Dana," said
Anthony sweetly. "I've come to give you
a present."

"A present?" said Dana.

"Come outside and see," said Anthony.

Dana stepped outside . . .

. . . and was amazed to see a big white elephant. It was beautiful. It had a long trunk and clean, bright tusks. Its toenails were painted Dana's favorite color.

Dana was surprised that Anthony
had gotten her a present. And such a
wonderful present; she had always wanted
an elephant. Dana would not have given
a birthday present to someone who called
her an ickaborse and pinched her and ate
the dessert out of her lunch.

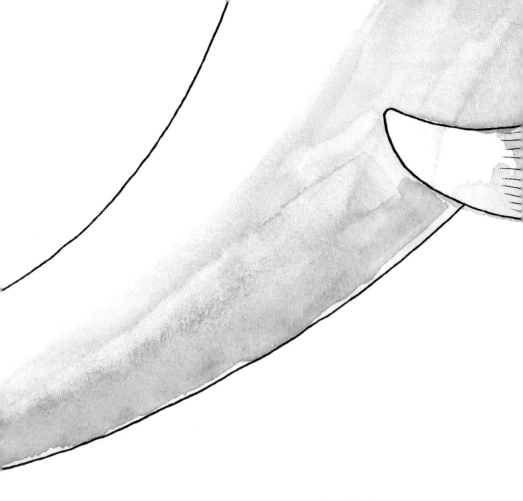

"Oh, my," said Dana. "I don't know what to say."

"Happy birthday, Dana," said Anthony. "Take good care of it."

"Of course," said Dana. She knew how important it is to take good care of one's pets.

Not Everyone Deserves an Elephant

Dana took the elephant for a walk around the block before bedtime. All the other kids were amazed and jealous.

"What a terrific elephant!" said the other kids.

"Yes," said Dana. "I got it for my birthday. It's probably the best elephant in the world."

"We wish we had an elephant like that," said the other kids.

"Oh, well," said Dana. "Not everyone deserves an elephant."

When they got back home, Dana took the big white elephant around to the back-yard. She spread a blanket out on the floor inside the shed, where they kept the lawn mower.

"There you go," she said. "Sleep tight."

The big white elephant looked at the shed and then looked at Dana. Dana felt ashamed. What was she thinking? Such a wonderful elephant couldn't sleep in a little old shed.

She took the big white elephant inside the house and put it in her bed.

"There," said Dana. "That's much better."

Dana lay down on the floor and thought about what a good friend Anthony had turned out to be, as the big white elephant's snores rattled the windows.

Grumble-Guts

In the morning, Dana made breakfast. She made
the big white elephant an especially big and tasty
breakfast, because it is important to take good
care of one's pets. The big white elephant ate
its breakfast. Then it looked at Dana.

"Of course," said Dana, "an elephant as big
and fine as you needs lots of food."

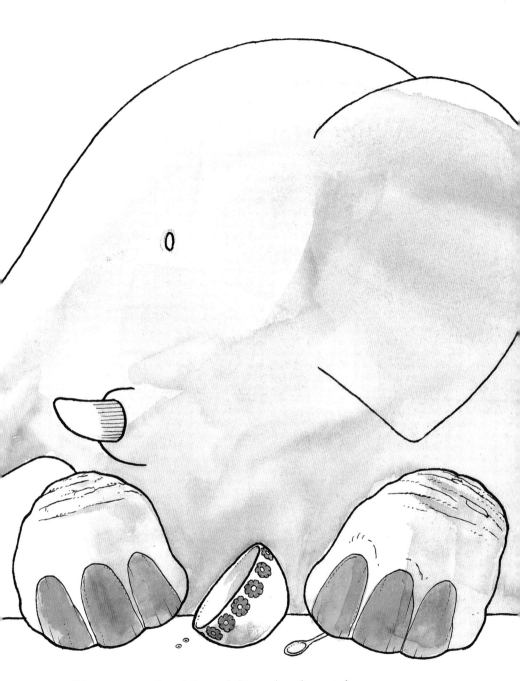

She gave the big white elephant her own
breakfast and it ate that, too.

Dana's stomach grumbled
all the way to school. Gertrude
called her Grumble-Guts on
the bus.

After school, Dana packed some snacks and took the big white elephant out for some exercise. The big white elephant walked and Dana rode Molly, her red ten-speed mountain bike.

They went for miles and miles, and still the big white elephant did not look tired. They went until Dana had to lie down for a bit. She had not slept well the night before, lying on the floor.

"You sure have a lot of energy," said Dana.

She unpacked their snacks. The big white elephant ate its snack. Then it ate Dana's snack. Then it looked at Molly.

"Would you like to ride Molly?" asked Dana.

The big white elephant *wumph*ed.

"Okay," said Dana, and she held the bike so the big white elephant could get on.

They walked back home.

Dana turned on the television for the elephant and took Molly to the bicycle repair shop.

"What a piece of junk," said Gertrude as Dana passed. Then Gertrude threw a mud ball at Dana.

Take Good Care

That night, Dana was so tired she could barely make dinner. The big white elephant ate its dinner and Dana's dinner and everything else in the refrigerator.

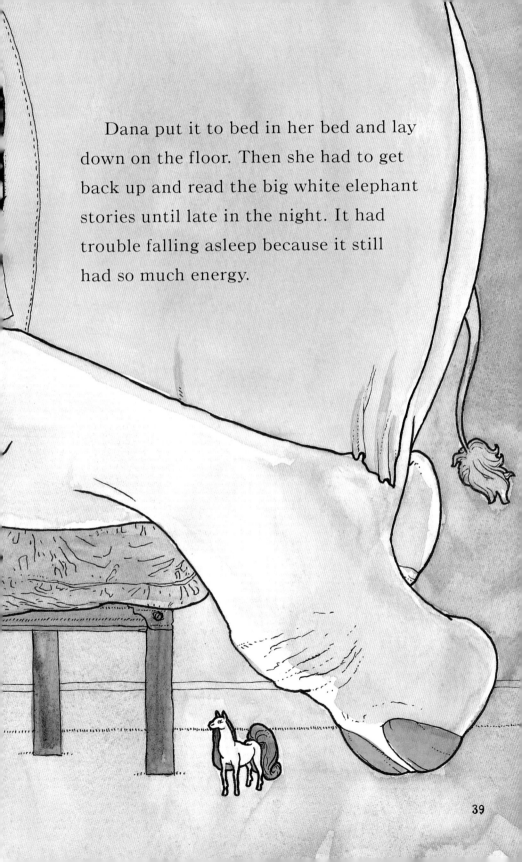

Dana put it to bed in her bed and lay
down on the floor. Then she had to get
back up and read the big white elephant
stories until late in the night. It had
trouble falling asleep because it still
had so much energy.

Dana woke up the next morning on the floor. She was at her wits' end. Taking care of the elephant was such hard work, and then Gertrude had called her names and thrown a mud ball at her on top of it. She felt terrible.

At school, Dana was so tired that she
nodded off during lunch, and Gertrude
ate her dessert.

Dana felt even worse. She thought about that for a while, then went over to Anthony's table.

"I'm sorry for calling you an ickaborse and pinching you and eating your dessert, Anthony," said Dana.

"Thank you," said Anthony. "Are you going to Gertrude's birthday party today?"

"I had forgotten that Gertrude's birthday was today," said Dana. She thought for a while.

After school, Dana gave
the big white elephant a bath.

She brushed the big white
elephant's tusks . . .

. . . and painted its toenails
Gertrude's favorite color.

Then she went to Gertrude's house.

Gertrude opened the door and looked at Dana suspiciously. "What do you want?"

"Happy birthday, Gertrude," said Dana sweetly. "I've come to give you a present."

She showed Gertrude the big white elephant.

"Oh, my," said Gertrude. "I don't know what to say."

"Happy birthday," said Dana. "Take good care of it."

The End